Look and Find Picture Puzzles

Princess Atta worries about having enough food for the grasshoppers.

Search the two pictures to find 10 things that are different.

For the solution, turn to page 110.

Look closely to find 10 differences in each pair of pictures! For the solutions to the puzzles, turn to the back of the book.

Published by
Louis Weber, C.E.O., Publications International, Ltd.
7373 North Cicero Avenue, Lincolnwood, Illinois 60712

Ground Floor, 59 Gloucester Place, London W1U 8JJ

Customer Service: 1-800-595-8484 or customer_service@pilbooks.com
www.pilbooks.com

p i kids is a registered trademark of Publications International, Ltd.

Look and Find is a registered trademark of Publications International, Ltd., in the United States and in Canada.

8 7 6 5 4 3 2 1

Manufactured in China.

ISBN-13: 978-1-60553-132-8
ISBN-10: 1-60553-132-4

Look and Find Picture Puzzles

publications international, ltd.

Andy plays with his favorite toys, Woody and Buzz.

Find 10 things that are different in the two pictures of Andy's room.

For the solution, turn to page 102.

Nemo loves his dad Marlin!

Search the two pictures to find 10 things that are different.

For the solution, turn to page 102.

When Carl was a little boy,
he discovered an old house.

Find 10 things that are different in the two pictures.

For the solution, turn to page 103.

Lightning McQueen helps his friend Mater at the junkyard.

Find 10 things that are different in the two pictures of Mater's junkyard.

For the solution, turn to page 103.

Remy, a rat with taste, loves to cook with vegetables.

Search the two pictures to find 10 things that are different.

For the solution, turn to page 104.

11

WALL-E shows off for his new friend EVE.

Find 10 differences in the two pictures of WALL-E's home.

For the solution, turn to page 104.

The Incredibles are a super family!

Search the two pictures to find 10 things that are different.

For the solution, turn to page 105.

Woody and the toys watch as Andy's birthday guests arrive.

Find 10 differences in the two pictures of Andy's toys.

For the solution, turn to page 105.

17

Nemo and his friends throw a party.

Search the two pictures to find 10 things that are different.

For the solution, turn to page 106.

Carl's house is surrounded by noisy construction.

Find 10 differences in the two pictures of Carl's house.

For the solution, turn to page 106.

Mater trails behind Lightning as they race around a bend.

Search the two pictures to find 10 things that are different.

For the solution, turn to page 107.

Woody spots Andy and his mom at Pizza Planet.

Find 10 differences in the two pictures of Pizza Planet.

For the solution, turn to page 107.

The circus performers and the grasshoppers arrive at Ant Island.

Search the two pictures to find 10 things that are different.

For the solution, turn to page 108.

Carl sits alone inside his house.

Find 10 differences in the two pictures of Carl's home.

Guido fits new tires on Mater at Luigi's shop.

Search the two pictures to find 10 things that are different.

Woody gathers the toys
for a staff meeting.

Search the two pictures of Andy's room to find 10 differences.

For the solution, turn to page 109.

33

Nemo and his friends have fun with Mr. Ray.

Search the two pictures to find 10 things that are different.

For the solution, turn to page 110.

Princess Atta worries about having enough food for the grasshoppers.

Search the two pictures to find 10 things that are different.

For the solution, turn to page 110.

Skinner pushes past Linguini and into the refrigerator.

Find 10 differences in the two pictures of the walk-in refrigerator.

For the solution, turn to page 111.

WALL-E wanders an abandoned street on Earth.

Search the two pictures to find 10 things that are different.

For the solution, turn to page 111.

Life is back to normal for the Parrs at Dash's track meet.

Find 10 differences in the two pictures of Dash's track meet.

For the solution, turn to page 112.

Woody and the mutant toys teach Sid a lesson.

Search the two pictures to find 10 things that are different.

For the solution, turn to page 112.

Nemo loves to swim with Dory.

Search the two pictures to find 10 things that are different.

For the solution, turn to page 113.

47

Carl's house goes up!

Search these two pictures to find 10 things that are different.

For the solution, turn to page 113.

Lightning and Mater visit Ramone's body shop.

Find 10 differences in the two pictures of Ramone's shop.

For the solution, turn to page 114.

Remy gives Linguini his first cooking lesson.

Search these pictures to find 10 things that are different.

For the solution, turn to page 114.

WALL-E gazes up at the signs onboard EVE's ship, the *Axiom.*

Search these pictures to find 10 things that are different.

For the solution, turn to page 115.

55

Dash and Violet disturb the Parrs' family dinner.

Find 10 differences in the two suppertime pictures.

For the solution, turn to page 115.

57

Oops! Woody ends up in a yard sale, where a man named Al finds him.

Find 10 differences in the two pictures of the yard sale.

Nemo and his friends untangle Sheldon from some seaweed.

Search these two pictures to find 10 things that are different.

For the solution, turn to page 116.

61

Carl walks his floating house through the jungle with Russell.

Search these two pictures to find 10 things that are different.

For the solution, turn to page 117.

Sheriff scolds Lightning for speeding on the highway.

Find 10 differences in the two pictures of the highway.

For the solution, turn to page 117.

At Al's apartment, Woody finds out he was once a big TV star!

Find 10 differences in the two pictures of Al's apartment.

For the solution, turn to page 118.

Marlin drops Nemo off at school.

Find 10 differences in the two pictures of Nemo's school.

For the solution, turn to page 118.

Carl and Russell meet Dug in the jungle.

Search these two pictures to find 10 things that are different.

For the solution, turn to page 119.

Buzz and his friends search for Woody in Al's Toy Barn.

Find 10 differences in the two pictures of the store.

The ants line up while Francis talks to his friends.

Search the two pictures and find 10 things that are different.

For the solution, turn to page 120.

Russell floats through the air using Carl's balloons.

Find 10 things that are different in the two pictures of Russell.

For the solution, turn to page 120.

Mater tows Lightning out of a ditch.

Search these two pictures to find 10 things that are different.

For the solution, turn to page 121.

Skinner chases after Remy, but splashes into the water instead!

Search these two pictures to find 10 things that are different.

For the solution, turn to page 121.

EVE comforts her friend WALL-E.

Search these two pictures to find 10 things that are different.

For the solution, turn to page 122.

The Incredibles and Frozone save the day!

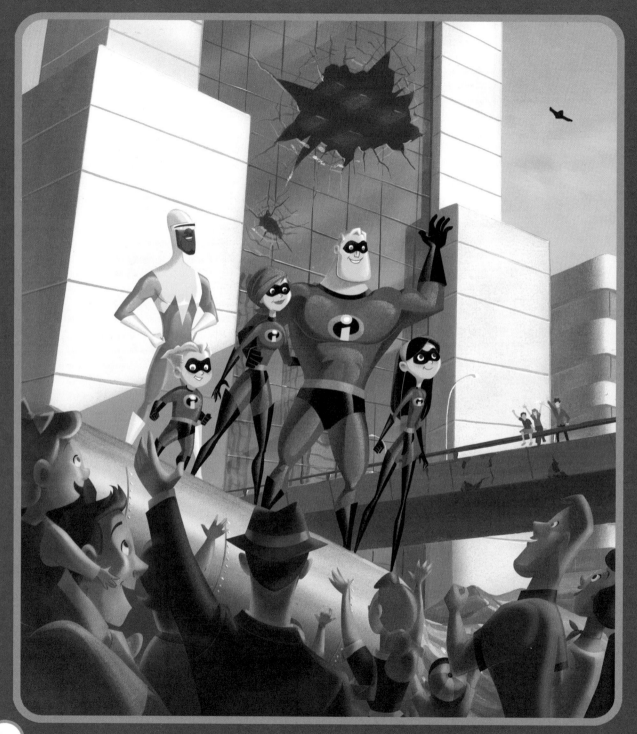

Find 10 differences in the two pictures of the Incredibles.

For the solution, turn to page 122.

Flik tries to hide the circus sign from the other ants.

Search these two pictures to find 10 things that are different.

For the solution, turn to page 123.

The sharks sing a fun song to their friends.

Search these two pictures to find 10 things that are different.

For the solution, turn to page 123.

Carl throws away his belongings to make the house lighter.

Search these two pictures to find 10 things that are different.

For the solution, turn to page 124.

Mater shows off his new look at Flo's V8 Cafe.

Find 10 differences in the two pictures of Flo's.

For the solution, turn to page 124.

Woody spins around a record player with Jessie and Bullseye.

Search these two pictures to find 10 things that are different.

For the solution, turn to page 125.

Nemo swims through some underwater traffic.

Search these two pictures to find 10 things that are different.

For the solution, turn to page 125.

Carl tries to stop Russell from leaving.

Search these two pictures to find 10 things that are different.

For the solution, turn to page 126.

Remy looks over the beautiful city of Paris.

Search these two pictures to find 10 things that are different.

For the solution, turn to page 126.

This is the answer key to the Picture Puzzle on pages 2 & 3.

This is the answer key to the Picture Puzzle on pages 4 & 5.

This is the answer key to the Picture Puzzle on pages 6 & 7.

This is the answer key to the Picture Puzzle on pages 8 & 9.

This is the answer key to the Picture Puzzle on pages 10 & 11.

This is the answer key to the Picture Puzzle on pages 12 & 13.

This is the answer key
to the Picture Puzzle
on pages 14 & 15.

This is the answer key
to the Picture Puzzle
on pages 16 & 17.

This is the answer key to the Picture Puzzle on pages 18 & 19.

This is the answer key to the Picture Puzzle on pages 20 & 21.

This is the answer key to the Picture Puzzle on pages 22 & 23.

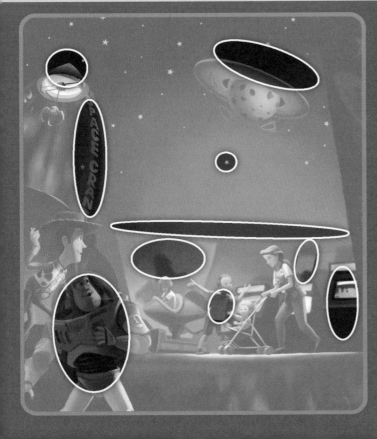

This is the answer key to the Picture Puzzle on pages 24 & 25.

This is the answer key to the Picture Puzzle on pages 26 & 27.

This is the answer key to the Picture Puzzle on pages 28 & 29.

This is the answer key
to the Picture Puzzle
on pages 30 & 31.

This is the answer key
to the Picture Puzzle
on pages 32 & 33.

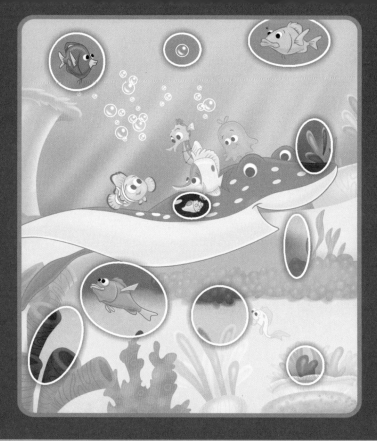

This is the answer key to the Picture Puzzle on pages 34 & 35.

This is the answer key to the Picture Puzzle on pages 36 & 37.

This is the answer key to the Picture Puzzle on pages 38 & 39.

This is the answer key to the Picture Puzzle on pages 40 & 41.

This is the answer key
to the Picture Puzzle
on pages 42 & 43.

This is the answer key
to the Picture Puzzle
on pages 44 & 45.

This is the answer key
to the Picture Puzzle
on pages 46 & 47.

This is the answer key
to the Picture Puzzle
on pages 48 & 49.

This is the answer key to the Picture Puzzle on pages 50 & 51.

This is the answer key to the Picture Puzzle on pages 52 & 53.

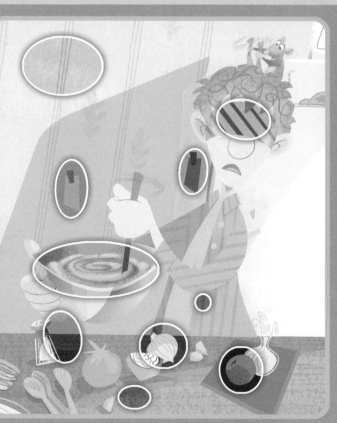

This is the answer key to the Picture Puzzle on pages 54 & 55.

This is the answer key to the Picture Puzzle on pages 56 & 57.

This is the answer key to the Picture Puzzle on pages 58 & 59.

This is the answer key to the Picture Puzzle on pages 60 & 61.

This is the answer key
to the Picture Puzzle
on pages 62 & 63.

This is the answer key
to the Picture Puzzle
on pages 64 & 65.

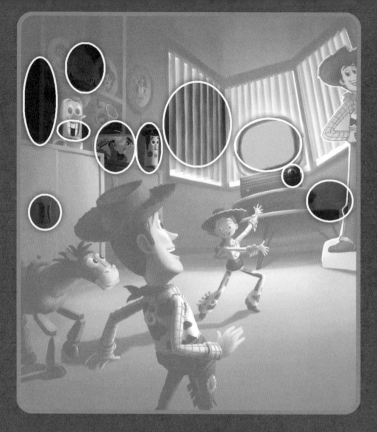

This is the answer key to the Picture Puzzle on pages 66 & 67.

This is the answer key to the Picture Puzzle on pages 68 & 69.

This is the answer key to the Picture Puzzle on pages 70 & 71.

This is the answer key to the Picture Puzzle on pages 72 & 73.

This is the answer key to the Picture Puzzle on pages 74 & 75.

This is the answer key to the Picture Puzzle on pages 76 & 77.

This is the answer key
to the Picture Puzzle
on pages 78 & 79.

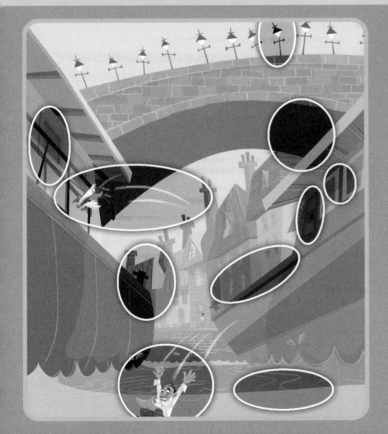

This is the answer key
to the Picture Puzzle
on pages 80 & 81.

This is the answer key
to the Picture Puzzle
on pages 82 & 83.

This is the answer key
to the Picture Puzzle
on pages 84 & 85.

This is the answer key
to the Picture Puzzle
on pages 86 & 87.

This is the answer key
to the Picture Puzzle
on pages 88 & 89.

This is the answer key to the Picture Puzzle on pages 90 & 91.

This is the answer key to the Picture Puzzle on pages 92 & 93.

This is the answer key to the Picture Puzzle on pages 94 & 95.

This is the answer key to the Picture Puzzle on pages 96 & 97.

This is the answer key to the Picture Puzzle on pages 98 & 99.

This is the answer key to the Picture Puzzle on pages 100 & 101.